THE BIKER'S REVENGE

UNDERGROUND CROWS MC BOOK ONE

SADIE KING

LET'S BE BESTIES!

A few times a month I send out an email with new releases, special deals and sneak peeks of what I'm working on. If you want to get on the list I'd love to meet you!

You'll even get a free short and steamy romance when you join.

Sign up here:
www.authorsadieking.com/free

THE BIKER'S REVENGE

UNDERGROUND CROWS MC

She's my enemy's daughter and my new obsession...

After three years inside, there's only one thing I want: revenge.

But when a retaliation goes wrong, I find myself with a fire cat captive—Scarlett, my enemy's daughter.

She's half my age and dripping with innocence. Scarlett becomes my revenge, and it's never been sweeter. But when her father comes for her, there's no way I'm giving her up.

The Biker's Revenge is a forbidden love, age-gap romance that starts with a kidnapping and ends with a happily ever after. Featuring an OTT obsessed hero and the curvy girl he claims as his own.

BRUNO

The sound of smashing glass breaks the silence. Pans shakes out the rag that he wrapped around his wrist to break the window, sending shards of glass tumbling to the ground.

My eyes dart around the shadowy building, my ears straining for any sign that someone is inside.

But all is quiet at the Chaos Riders HQ. Our intel was correct. The club is on a run out of town, leaving their headquarters unprotected.

I don't expect to find much here, but we'll rough the place up, do as much damage as possible. I want Manny, the Chaos Riders' president, to know that I'm out, and I'm out for revenge.

I give a signal to the boys, and dark shapes emerge from the shadows. Pans is the first one in the window, and he clears the glass with a covered fist so no one gets cut as we climb through.

Flashing lights from the neon sign out front illuminate a bar with dancing poles leading up to the ceiling.

Lyle whistles. "Could get one of those installed at our place, Pres."

I shoot him a dark look. "You keep that in the strip club."

Lyle grins, but he knows I'm serious. My club is a place that's safe for women. There's a time and a place for a strip pole, and it's not front and center of our MC club.

"Where should we start?"

Jesse whistles softly as he twirls a baseball bat in his hand.

It's been a long time since I've been inside the Chaos Riders' clubrooms. It's been years since we were on friendly terms.

The floor's sticky, and empty beer bottles lay scattered on the floor. A thick layer of dust coats the framed pictures of bikes on the walls. The place stinks of vomit and stale beer, making my nose crinkle.

They don't take pride in their clubhouse the way we do. Maybe this little visit isn't going to hurt them too badly. But it's not about hurting them. It's about letting Manny know we're coming for him, letting him know that I'm out and I want my revenge.

"Anywhere you like. Smash it all to hell."

I swing my bat at the wall, feeling a surge of satisfaction as a portrait of Manny crashes to the ground.

The glass frame shatters, and I don't bother trying to muffle the sound.

The boys let out a whoop and let loose with their bats, swinging wildly at anything and everything.

I reckon we've got about five minutes before someone shows up, and I'm not going to waste that time.

Pulling my shoulder back, I swing as hard as I can,

connecting with a pinball machine. It gives a strangled beep as the glass smashes. I hit it again and again, thinking about the last three years. Three years in prison, locked up and away from my club and away from my daughter, Lily.

It's lucky I had the foresight to add Gina as one of her guardians. I did that ten years ago in case something ever happened to me so they couldn't take my daughter away. My bat comes down on the legs of the pinball machine, and it gives a whine as a leg gives out and it sinks to its knees.

Smashing shit up feels good. I spin around, looking for my next target.

The room is in chaos with my guys joyfully destroying the clubhouse.

Lyle has rescued a bottle of bourbon from the bar, and he takes a swig before smashing the fridges in.

Someone's gone through to the kitchen, and there's the sound of pots and pans being thrown to the floor.

There's a staircase, and I head up there. I'm looking for the President's room. I want to destroy something that belongs to the man who put me behind bars, that made me miss out on so much of Lily's life.

"That's for missing her prom."

I swing the bat heavily, getting grim satisfaction as it carves a hole in the plaster of the wall.

"And that's for missing her high school graduation."

The bat makes another hole, and this feels fucking good. Manny put me behind bars. He snitched on me. I was supposed to meet him and his crew for an arms deal. Instead, the cops turned up and caught me with a trunk full of illegal firearms.

I only got a lesser sentence because my sister is the best lawyer in the state.

There's a corridor upstairs with doors leading off to rooms. I try each one, looking for something that Manny would value.

There's a small cupboard at the end, and it's the only door that's locked, which means there must be something worth protecting in there.

I swing my bat hard. It wedges in the door, sending a jolt up my shoulder.

"Motherfucker."

I pull the bat out and swing again. This time, it goes all the way through, making a hole in the door. I reach my hand through, searching for the lock on the other side. My hand finds the doorknob and I turn it, hearing the lock pop open.

There's a rushing sound from the other side of the door, and something comes down on my hand, sending pain shooting up my arm.

"Fuck!" I pull my hand out, and there's blood on my knuckles. Pain sears up my arm, and I see red. Whoever's behind that door is going to pay for this.

My fingers are bent in pain, and I can't grip the baseball bat properly, but I raise it as best I can and open the door.

Someone rushes me. A small ball of fury, hissing at me, all hair and nails, scratching at my arms as they knock me off balance. I step back, pinned against the other side of the corridor. My bat drops to the floor as I wrestle with the wild cat that's tearing at my skin with her nails.

I know it's a woman because she smells good. Her long

hair is wild, and every time it whips around my face, I get a whiff of the floral scent of whatever shampoo she uses.

She's got her legs wrapped around me while her fingers claw at my neck. My head tilts back so she can't scratch my face, and I use my arms to try to wrestle her off. But with my injured hand, it's hard to get a grip on her.

She's fighting with everything she's got, like a cornered animal.

"I'm not gonna hurt you."

I try to calm her down, but it only makes her more irate. I don't want to hurt her, but I need to get her off me before she finds an eyeball with one of those nails.

"I need you to calm down."

I try to warn her, but she still gives a surprised oomph when I drop to my knees and roll her onto the floor.

Now I'm pinning her down, holding her still with my one good arm. Her hair falls off her face, and for the first time, I get a proper look at my attacker.

She's got full, youthful lips, deep red where she's been biting them. Her skin is smooth and tanned, and her wide, dark eyes cast around the room wildly.

My breath catches in my throat. My blood roars in my ears.

Mine.

The word echoes in my head, pounds in my heart, and reverberates through my very soul.

Mine, Mine, Mine.

It's a clear chant in my head that I'm sure she must hear. And maybe she does because her eyes find mine. She stills for a moment, and we stare at each other.

Her look is pure terror, and a flash of anger goes through me, wondering what she's so frightened of.

"I'm not going to hurt you."

I keep my voice steady and calm, like how you'd talk to a frightened animal, and it seems to work.

Her eyes stay on me, and her breathing slows. I can feel the swell of her breasts under me with each ragged breath. And help me, God, but I can't help but glance down to peek at the soft mounds that are billowing up and down as she breathes.

Her top has come unbuttoned, and the white lace of her bra is on show, framing two soft pillowy breasts.

My body responds instantly. And she must feel it because the fight comes back into her. She kicks her knee up, and I duck out the way before she can get me in the goods.

The woman rolls out from under me, and I grab her by the ankle before she can escape. She gives a whimper as I drag her back and pin her under me again.

This time, I pin her legs down with my thighs as I hold her hands over her head.

She looks beautiful splayed out on the ground. More than beautiful. The blood in my veins rushes south, and I have to look away. I have to block the sight of her below me, the scent of her filling my nostrils. Because I'm not an animal and because I recognize this girl. Although she's not a girl anymore, now clearly a woman. She's Scarlett, Manny's daughter.

"I'm not going to hurt you, Scarlett."

Her eyes widen when I say her name, and her nostrils flare. "My father will find you."

6

She spits the words with such venom that spittle lands on my lips. I flick my tongue out, tasting her on me. Salty and sweet.

"I'm counting on it."

She breathes hard, but when I help her to her feet, she doesn't resist.

Keeping one hand grasped around Scarlett's wrists, I look into what I thought was a closet, the room where Scarlett was hiding. There's a mattress on the floor and a shelf with a few books and a small stack of folded clothes.

"This your room?"

She sticks her chin out defiantly, not giving me an answer. But the way her cheeks flush red tells me everything I need to know.

Manny lets his daughter sleep in a closet. The guy doesn't deserve her.

The sounds of crashing from downstairs have faded, and Jesse appears at the top of the stairs. "Time to go, Pres."

"I guess I'll be the one who has to clean this mess up," Scarlett huffs.

"Not this time, darling."

I lift her off her feet, and she gives a squeal. She's curvy but she's short, and I toss her over my shoulder like a sack of potatoes.

"What are you doing?" Scarlett gives an indignant huff.

I don't answer her because it's obvious what I'm doing. I'm taking her.

"Put me down." Scarlett wriggles on my shoulder, and her small fists pummel my back. I stride down the stairs to where the guys are waiting.

"Who's the girl?" Lyle asks.

I wrap my arms around Scarlett's jean-clad thighs, pinning her in place.

"She's my revenge."

2

SCARLETT

I'm tied to him. I'm actually fucking tied to him.

As if it wasn't brutal enough to break into the clubhouse and kidnap me. Now a thick rope binds me to him as we speed down the highway on the back of his motorbike.

They had a van. They could have thrown me in the back, but this brute decided he'd rather tie me up.

I'm not scared we'll have an accident. I've been riding since before I could walk. And even though this guy's a brute, I feel safe on the back of his bike.

I'm pressed up against him so close that I can smell his leathers and musky scent. My arms are forced around his waist, and my cheek presses against the back of his biker jacket. I'm pressed so close I'll probably have "Underground Crows MC" emblazoned on my cheek.

Maybe that's what Bruno wants. I knew who he was the moment I saw him. I've known my father's enemies my whole life.

They were friends once, Dad and Bruno. I used to play

with his daughter. But that was a long time ago, before whatever dealings got in the way and made them rivals.

My dad will be furious when he finds out what they've done. I should have gone with the club out of town, but I volunteered to stay and clean the clubhouse. I'd rather clean up old beer and vomit than go drinking with the club.

I'd have to stay sober and watch myself and make sure I'm never alone in case one of the bikers cornered me and tried to kiss me…or worse.

Which is probably what Bruno's got planned. That's the ultimate revenge, isn't it? Ravage the women of your rival?

Panic sweeps through me, and I pull at the bindings on my hands. The bike swerves, and Bruno slows down but doesn't stop.

He probably knows I don't have a move here. What am I going to do? Cause us to have an accident?

My mind whirs at the possibilities. I suppose we'd skid and fall off, and I'm wearing a helmet so I might be okay, or I might not. But that would be better than being ravaged by this brute. *Would it, though?* My body whispers.

I shake the thought aside and try to forget the tug in my core that I felt when Bruno pinned me down, the way my nipples have been hard ever since he threw me over his shoulder, and the fact that as we ride down the freeway, my thighs pressed tight against him, there's a damp heat building in my panties.

It's just the vibrations of the bike, I tell myself.

Bruno's of the same ilk as my father. He's hard and cold, and even though he feels safe, I can't trust him. I need to do whatever I can to escape, to get away from him and back to my father.

. . .

It's another twenty minutes before the bike slows and we pull into what I assume is the Underground Crows HQ.

The tang of salt hangs on the air, and the sounds of waves crashing against concrete lets me know we're right on the water's edge.

Bruno kills the engine and takes his helmet off.

"If I untie this rope, are you gonna run?"

I glance around, not sure yet what I'll do. At one end of the parking lot is a building with a neon sign announcing, "Girls, girls, girls."

The Crows own a strip bar. Charming. That tells me everything I need to know about these men, that they're just like the men at my club. They believe women are only here for one thing. Two if you count cleaning.

The club compound is surrounded on two sides by water. Because I'm my father's daughter, my first thought is about how that limits your escape options. Until I see dark shapes lined up and bobbing in the water. It seems the Crows keep a contingent of boats and jet skis. Either they love being out on the ocean, or they've got one hell of a getaway plan.

The other guys are pulling up alongside the Pres, and after the van pulls in, someone rushes out to shut the gate. I'm shut in, with iron gates on one side and the ocean on the other. There's nowhere to run to.

"No." I shake my head. Because where would I go?

Bruno unties the rope that has my arms around him, and I pull my hands back. They ache with stiffness, and I rub them, trying to get the blood flowing.

Bruno gets off the bike, and my body immediately misses his warmth. Treacherous body.

He offers a hand, but I brush past him as I swing my leg over and off the bike. If there's one thing I know how to handle, it's a bike—which gives me an idea.

A jet ski is really just a bike on the water. If I can get to one, I'm pretty sure I could ride it. And if they're lined up and ready for a getaway, I'd bet money that the keys are in them.

That's what my dad would do.

"You okay?"

Bruno's gaze is intense, and I get the feeling that it's not just a courtesy check-in. He really wants to know if I'm okay.

There're scratch marks on his face and a trickle of blood on his cheek, and I'm proud that I put them there, but also feel a little bad for him, which is stupid. He kidnapped me.

The reminder of how we got here sends a fresh bolt of anger through me, and I want to scratch him again. But I force myself to look defeated. Let him think that I'm cowed.

"I'm fine," I say, rubbing the blood back into my arms.

He turns to speak to the guys coming in on their bikes. Now's my chance.

I take off, heading for the water and the jet skis.

There's a shout behind me and the pounding of feet, but I daren't look back. I'm almost at the water, and if I can't make it to the jet skis, I'll just throw myself into the ocean.

My heart is hammering in my chest. I've never run so fast in my life. The footsteps get louder and then strong arms are around me. I'm being lifted off my feet, and I kick them wildly, not caring what I connect with.

"Let me go!"

But Bruno just tightens his grip. I know it's him because I already recognize his distinct smell, and his voice is deep when he speaks barely over a whisper. It makes my whole body shiver.

"Never."

Then he's got me over his shoulder again, and I pound his back as he carries me into the clubhouse and up the stairs.

He carries me into a room and deposits me on the bed. The sheets are plush and silky, and even though I should be scared, I can't help admiring how much nicer this clubhouse is than ours. I sit on the bed, and Bruno kneels before me and grips my shoulders like he's talking to a child. And I guess that's what he thinks I am. A child. That shouldn't disappoint me, but it does.

"I'm not going to hurt you, Scarlett. You've got to believe me."

I want to believe him, but why else would he kidnap me and bring me into a bedroom with plush sheets if it wasn't to let the club loose on me?

I shiver at the thought, and a flash of confusion crosses his face.

"You don't have to be scared here, honey. No one's going to hurt you."

He says it slowly, and a part of me starts to think that maybe it's true.

"No one's going to hurt you, but you've got to stop fighting me, okay?"

I nod my head because he wants me to believe him, and maybe if I go along with it, I'll find a way to escape.

"I'm going to leave you here to calm down. I'll bring some food up to you soon. Make yourself comfortable."

He leaves the room, and as he shuts the door, there's a clinking sound that lets me know he's locked the door.

I get up and try it anyway, but sure enough, it's locked.

A quick tour of the room shows a window that leads to a dark alleyway. I open it and lean out, but I can't see how far down it is or what's below.

There's a small bathroom off the bedroom, but the window in there is too small for the likes of me to squeeze through.

I go back to the bed and flop onto it. The memory foam mattress molds to my body, and it's so much comfier than the lumpy mattress on the floor that I usually sleep on.

The covers are satin, and I run them over my cheek, enjoying the silky feel against my skin. I bet that feels good on your body.

My body suddenly feels heavy, the adrenaline from the last hour draining away. I need to escape, but first, I'll just see what it feels like to lie down in a soft bed with a comfy mattress.

I'm Bruno's prisoner, for now. But I may as well enjoy a good night's sleep in a plush bed while I'm here.

3

BRUNO

*M*y skin stings where Scarlett scratched me, and there's bruising on my knuckles. A surge of pride goes through me that she fought so hard. She's a firecracker, that's for sure, and I'm proud to wear her marks.

I hate to leave Scarlett in the room alone, but she needs time to calm down and I need a debrief with the guys.

There're cheers and raised beer bottles when I enter the room downstairs. Gage slaps me on the back, a wide grin peeking out from under his beard.

"If Manny didn't know you're out, then he does now."

Lyle hands me a beer and I clink bottles, but I can't put a grin on my face. All I can think about is Scarlett, her soft body under mine, and the implications of what I already know to be true. She's mine, and I'll start a gang war over her if I have to.

But there's something else that's troubling me. The terrified look on her face. How she doesn't believe I'll keep her safe. What's got her so frightened?

Jesse is the only one not smiling. He leans against the bar with his arms folded.

"You got to return the girl."

It's just like Jesse to be blunt. While everyone else is celebrating my victory, he's brooding over the consequences. That's why he's my VP.

"Church. Now," I command.

Beer bottles are set down reluctantly, and the group shuffles into the room next to the bar where we talk club business. Not that there's anyone else here at this time of night, but I need the club to understand where I stand on this.

Once everyone's seated, I look around at my club. It's only the second time we've sat around the table since I got out of prison yesterday.

I take a moment to appreciate my crew because, yeah, I missed their ugly mugs when I was inside.

Jesse has his arms folded, serious and brooding. Some people think he's a miserable motherfucker, but he's a deep thinker and loyal to the grave.

Lyle is the pretty boy of the group with his cropped blonde hair and clean-shaven face. He's ex-military and works outside the club in security.

His leg bounces up and down as he spins a bottle top on the table. Lyle can never sit still since he came back from service. He's the joker of the group and the one we send out as our public face. He's kindhearted, and he's here because he needs a family and he believes in the good we do in this community.

Gage sinks into his chair, and it creaks under his weight. He's the biggest of our crew. Six foot five and as wide as he is tall, with an impressive beard and an easy grin. But don't let the rough exterior fool you. Gage is smart, sharp as a tack, and can spot a phony a mile away. He gets shit because when he's on shift at the strip club, he sits in the corner reading a fucking book.

Quinn drums his finger on the table, his wedding ring knocking against the wood. He recently married a law student from Temptation Bay and is most definitely pussy-whipped. She's away finishing her studies, and they talk on the phone every night like lovesick teenagers.

Kray's the same. His woman moved here recently from Sycamore Mountain with some scheme about helping local orphans. He came to us for the cash to fund the program. It was agreed to while I was inside, and I approve. We may do some shit that's not completely legit, but ultimately, we want to do good in the community.

We've got a legit business in the strip club, and Jesse is pushing to get us out of the gun business. But guns are what I know. Three years inside didn't change my mind about that.

Then there's Pans, sullen and brooding, and this time it's not covering a thoughtful inner life. Pans is ex-military too, and somewhere in the depths of Afghanistan, he lost himself. He's got a darkness in him that terrifies even me sometimes.

His dark eyes focus on a spot on the table, and his hand shoots out to stop Quinn's tapping, his red-scarred hand engulfing Quinn's. Their eyes meet, and after an intense beat, Quinn pulls back.

"All right, keep your hair on," Quinn mutters. "You're just jealous because you haven't got a woman."

God help the woman who takes on Pans' dead heart. He's more of a cold-hearted bastard than I am.

These are my men, my brothers. I'd die for these guys, every single one of them.

"Nice touch with the girl," Lyle says. "But when are we taking her back?"

There're murmurs of ascent around the table, and it's my turn to drum my fingers patiently because these guys don't get it yet.

"I'm not taking her back."

Jesse shakes his head slowly. "We got to take her back, Pres. She's Manny's daughter."

My fists tighten and a vein throbs in my neck at the thought of handing Scarlett back.

"It could start a war with the Chaos Riders," says Gage.

My mind goes to Scarlett's soft body, to her heaving breasts, to her plump lips aching to be kissed. Let them start a war. I'll kill every single man in the Chaos Riders for her.

"No." I say it firmly, my fist thumping on the table. "I'm keeping her."

There's the shaking of heads, and no one can look me in the eye. Except Jesse.

"You can't keep her against her will. That's not how we treat women."

I hate that the son of a bitch is right. We may own a strip club, but we're good to our women. We treat them with respect and protect them as we would any of our brothers.

"Then I'll make her want to stay." My hand grips the table, and I realize I'm acting like a petulant child with a new toy. But I'm not giving Scarlett up.

The men don't agree with me, and someone mutters

about women being trouble, but they don't get it yet. I'm already in trouble. Scarlett owns me, and there's nothing I won't do for her.

"Is she worth starting a war over?" Jesse asks.

I'm not even going to answer that because she is. I'd burn the whole fucking coast down for Scarlett.

"Scarlett stays with us."

I slam the gavel down, signaling that this discussion is over. I'm not even voting on this one. Scarlett is staying, and that's the final decision.

4

SCARLETT

*S*unlight flickers across my face, pulling me out of a deep sleep. I can't remember the last time I slept so deeply. I'm usually woken by drunk voices outside my door and the rattling of my lock.

It must mean that Dad's back. The club members leave me alone when he's around. Most of the guys respect him enough to leave me alone all the time, but there're a few assholes in the club that stare at me in a way that makes me uncomfortable, they say nasty things and lunge for me every time they drink.

Memories of last night flash through my mind. The clubhouse being destroyed, Bruno pinning me down, Bruno tying me up, Bruno carrying me over his shoulder. Bruno, Bruno, Bruno.

I sit up with a start, the last blanket of sleep crashing around me.

I'm not in my box room at the clubhouse. I'm at the Underground Crows clubhouse, and I'm Bruno's prisoner.

My gaze darts around the room. The rest of the furniture is as plush as the bed. A dark mahogany dresser sits in one corner, an armchair in another. It's nice, homely, and tidy, much nicer than the rooms back at my clubhouse. But I'm not here to admire the decor. I need to get out of here before someone comes back and does God knows what to me.

I push myself out of bed and to the window.

In the darkness last night, I couldn't see where the drop leads. But in the daylight, I see some empty crates and a keg of beer. There's nowhere for a soft landing.

I'm about to try the bathroom again when I hear a key turn in a lock. The thought that Bruno's on the other side of the door makes me hesitate.

He's not like the guys at my MC, I can tell. He says he won't hurt me, and I believe him, but it's more than that. When I was pinned under him last night, when I saw the flash of desire in his eyes, I wanted him too.

But I push that aside. I'm half his age and his rival's daughter. I must be mad to be having naughty thoughts about the Underground Crows' president.

The door handle starts to turn. It's now or never. Flinging open the window, I swing my leg over the sill.

"Hey!"

Bruno's gravelly voice almost makes me stop, but I push on. I can't let my feelings for him cloud my judgement. Who knows what his men will do to me... I have to get out of here.

I swing my other leg over the windowsill, mutter a quick prayer to whoever's listening, and jump.

The concrete comes up quickly, and I land half on a

crate and half on the hard ground. Pain shoots up my ankle as it twists under me.

"Scarlett!" The fury in Bruno's voice makes my bones rattle. I glance up, and he's leaning out of the window. But it's not anger on his face. It's pure terror.

We stare at each other, my breath ragged. I should run, but I'm transfixed by the intensity of his gaze, wondering what he's so frightened of. I didn't think anything could scare Bruno.

"I'm coming for you."

He ducks away from the window. I imagine him thundering across the landing and down the stairs. I have a few seconds to get away, and I should run. I should get up and run.

"Get up, girl," I grit out between my teeth. But when I push up off the ground, pain shoots up my ankle.

"Fuuuuck!" I crumple on the ground, holding my ankle, my eyes squeezed tight against the pain. And that's how Bruno finds me a few moments later.

"Are you hurt? Are you bleeding?"

The concern on his face is genuine, and without waiting for an answer, his hands are on me. With a gentleness that belies his huge frame, Bruno checks me over, his hands running up my spine, over my hips and my shoulders, checking for injuries.

"My ankle."

His hands press my ankle, and I wince at the pain.

"It's sprained."

The terror subsides as he realizes I'm still in one piece.

"You scared me, Scarlett. I thought you'd really hurt yourself."

There's relief in his voice. Does that mean he cares for me? Or is he just worried that I might kill myself before he can use me as a bargaining chip?

Bruno's arms slide around my waist, and he hoists me into his arms. I'm not a small girl. I'm short and dumpy. But in Bruno's arms, I feel light as a feather.

He carries me through the clubhouse, and this time, I lean into him, enjoying the solidness of him and the comfort it brings.

"Get ice."

Bruno calls instructions as he carries me up the stairs and back to the room. He sets me down carefully in the armchair and pulls a stool over for my leg.

A big guy with a beard and kind eyes brings in a bag of ice and a dish cloth. Then he leaves us alone.

Bruno slides off my shoe and the sock underneath. His touch is tender as his fingers caress the arch of my foot, and I pull back, giggling.

"That tickles."

The corner of his mouth twitches. "I had to check that you still have feeling in your feet."

"I can feel it hurting."

He wraps ice in the dishcloth and drapes it over my ankle.

"It's a sprain. You need to keep it elevated, let it rest."

I nod because this is so surreal, the president of the Underground Crows nursing my injured ankle.

"Do you really want to get away from me that badly?"

Bruno's hand is holding the ice in place, and his fingers graze my leg, sending shots of heat up my body.

I glance at him quickly, not sure if his touch was intentional.

The way he's looking at me makes my cheeks heat. He's intense, his chiseled features set with deep lines showing off a life well lived. The flecks of silver in his hair give him a commanding look, and I'm ready to be commandeered. I'll do anything he asks just to keep those eyes on me.

I've dated a few guys over the last few years, but no one gives me shivers the way Bruno does.

"Not you," I say because it's true. I know Bruno wouldn't hurt me.

"Then what are you so scared of, Scarlett?"

I lower my eyes because this is hard. I've seen what behavior goes on in clubs, what's expected of the women.

When I don't answer, Bruno takes my chin in his hand and tips my head up so I'm looking at him

"I'm not gonna hurt you, Scarlett."

"I know." I take a deep breath in. "It's not you I'm worried about."

5

BRUNO

*H*er words send a cold shiver down my spine. No woman should live in fear of men.

"You think my men would hurt you?"

It seems incredulous to me. We have a code of honor here. Women are to be looked after and protected. No man in my MC would ever lay a hand on a woman or take her by force. He'd be out the door and six feet under if he did.

Scarlett looks up at me with world-wary eyes, and I want to kill the motherfucker who took the innocence out of her heart.

"I've grown up in an MC, remember? I know what goes on."

Slow anger builds in my veins. If anyone's laid a finger on my girl without her consent, they'll pay.

"That doesn't go on in this club."

It comes out as a growl, and Scarlett startles. I stand up because I don't want to scare her with my intensity. But if anyone so much as looks at her sideways, they'll pay.

She shakes her head slightly, unbelieving. "I know what MC men are like…"

"Not my men."

My fist thumps on the dresser, and she jumps.

"I'm sorry… I didn't mean…"

She thinks I'm cross at her, but I'm not. I'm angry that this is her truth, that this is what she believes is going to happen to her here. I will my anger away and crouch down so I'm facing Scarlett.

"I'm not cross at you, honey. I'm cross at the mother-fuckers who made you so scared."

I take her hand in mine. It's small compared to my rough one, and I'm still hurting from the blow she landed on me, but I curl my fingers around hers, ignoring the ache in my knuckles.

"Did anyone…?" I can't even finish my sentence because I'm too scared of the answer.

"No." She shakes her head firmly. "I keep my door locked every night."

Fuck. This girl's been through hell, living in the lion's den in that cupboard she calls a room. I imagine her in there, cowering while drunk assholes try to get to her.

What the fuck was her dad doing not protecting his daughter? If any man so much as looks at my daughter, I'll rip their fucking eyes out.

Scarlett's staring at me with wide eyes. The fire from last night has gone out, and here's the vulnerable girl underneath, the woman who needs protection.

"Here."

I slide my cut off and hold it out for her. It's the best protection I can give her.

"Wear this and no one will touch you."

She hesitates. Her wide eyes find mine, and there's a question in them. Scarlett's grown up in an MC. She knows what it means when a man gives a woman his cut.

"Are you sure?"

I don't answer. I want to tell her how sure I am, but I don't want to scare her. Instead, I help her slide her arms into my jacket. It's big on her, but it looks good.

There's a rumbling noise, and Scarlett clutches her stomach, her cheeks flushing pink.

"You hungry?"

She winces in embarrassment. "I guess so."

"How do you like your eggs?"

She raises her eyebrows at me. "Don't tell me the president of the Crows cooks his own breakfast?"

I crack a smile at her sass. "Nope. But Gina should be here by now, and she makes a mean breakfast."

"Who's Gina?"

The smile drops from her face and her eyes narrow.

"You jealous, honey?"

Scarlett turns away quickly. "No."

I chuckle because if she's jealous, it means she cares and I'm the luckiest fucking guy in the world.

"Relax. Gina's like a sister to me. She runs the bar and looks after us."

Scarlett pushes her lower lip out, and God help me, I can't resist. I dart forward and capture her lips in mine.

The shock freezes her, then she's kissing me back. Her soft, plump lips are the sweetest thing I've ever tasted.

My hand snakes around her neck. I'm going to hell for

this, making out with my enemy's daughter, but I couldn't stop if all the hounds of hell were after me.

"Pres…" There's a knock at the door and I pull away. Lyle's wearing a smug look, which lets me know he caught us kissing.

"What is it?" I growl.

I want to be exploring Scarlett's mouth, running my hands over her tits, and finding out how tight that kitty cat between her legs is.

"We need you. It's urgent."

My need for Scarlett is urgent too. But she's wide-eyed and dazed, looking confused and lusty from our kiss. Fuck. I want to give her more than a kiss, but it's better I take my time with her, give her a chance to catch up. Because she doesn't yet know what I do—that we're meant to be together.

"I'll be back soon, sweetheart. Rest that foot, and no more escaping."

"I promise."

Reluctantly, I pull myself away and head downstairs to deal with club business.

6

SCARLETT

*M*y ankle throbs, and every time I try to move it, pain shoots up my leg. I don't know if Bruno locked the door when he left, but I'm not going anywhere. Though I'm starting to think that's fine by me.

Gina stopped by earlier with some breakfast and handed me a stack of romance novels. I've got to say, sitting in a nice clean room with my feet up isn't so bad. If I was back at my clubhouse, I'd be cleaning out the toilets or scrubbing vomit off the floor.

My thoughts wander to Bruno and the kiss we shared this morning. My lips tingle at the memory of his rough lips on mine. It felt good. Too good.

Ever since his mouth explored mine, I've had a sensation in my core, a tugging feeling that's making me restless. I want Bruno to come back. I want to keep kissing him. I want to find out where his hands were going before we were interrupted.

There's a knock at the door and my stomach flutters. But it's not Bruno that comes into the room.

It's been a long time since I saw Lily, but she hasn't changed a bit. She's tall, like her father with his same dark hair, but her bright green eyes must come from her mother.

"Hey," she says shyly, "I heard you were here."

Lily and I used to play together back when our dads were friends—or at least had a peaceful truce—but that was a long time ago.

Her eyes go wide when she sees my ankle. "What happened?"

I should be wary of Lily. I can't forget she's the president's daughter, but I find myself liking her immediately.

"I twisted it when I jumped out the window."

Her brows knit together as she puts two and two together. "Are you being held here against your will?"

I love her for the indignation in her voice. She puts her hands on her hips, and I get the feeling that Lily may look like sweetness and sunshine but there's a steel rod in her spine.

"It's okay," I tell her, and I realize I mean it. "I kinda like it here."

She eyes me, taking me in properly for the first time. Her hands run over the sleeve of her dad's jacket.

"He's given you his cut." She says it reverently, and I know she realizes the significance too. But maybe it's just a woman thing because Bruno seemed to hand it over like it was no big deal.

I shrug my shoulders like it's no big deal to me either. "I was cold."

Lily raises her eyebrows at me.

"Dad wouldn't even lend *me* his jacket if I was cold."

Her words make my heart jump. Maybe Bruno really is into me.

"There's only two women I've ever seen wear this cut. One was my mother, and the other is you."

At the mention of her mother, Lily goes quiet. She perches on the stool and takes my ankle carefully in her hands.

"What happened to your mother?" I can't help blurting out. It's probably rude to ask, but I'm desperate to know what happened to Bruno's old lady.

Lily unwraps the dishcloth with precise fingers and drops the melted ice into a bowl.

"She died."

"I'm sorry. I didn't mean to pry. It's none of my business."

Lily gives me a small smile. "It's okay. It was a long time ago. I was four. She had an aggressive form of cancer."

She grabs a dry dishcloth and re-wraps the ankle.

"I'm sorry."

It's a terrible thing to lose a mother. I should know. Mine ran off when I was a baby. She couldn't handle club life but didn't think to take me with her.

"It was hard at the time. Dad went nuts," Lily says.

It must have been about the time we stopped playing together, about the same time our clubs became rivals. I don't have many memories of Bruno from my childhood, but I wonder if he was always this hard.

"He hasn't shown any interest in another woman until now."

She smiles at me as she says the words, and my heart

does a happy flip. I'm that woman. I'm the woman that he's interested in.

"But I'm Manny's daughter."

Lily's eyes sparkle as she laughs.

"You think that'll stop my dad? Scarlett, if he's given you his cut, then you're already his."

She fusses over my ankle, and I sit in silence, warmth rushing through my heart. I'm already Bruno's, and I like it.

7

BRUNO

*M*y bike hums under me, and the wind whips across my face, the fresh, salty air stinging my eyelids. It's good to be on the road again, but I'm impatient to get back to the clubhouse.

We're heading back down the coast, and I'm going faster than I should, speeding to get back to Scarlett. It's agony being away from her, from her ripe lips and dark eyes.

Even in prison the days never felt this long.

We pull into the clubhouse and I'm off my bike like a rocket. It's dark already, and I hope Lily's been keeping her entertained like I asked.

I take the stairs two at a time and find them in the TV room laughing over some old sitcom. Scarlett's got her ankle resting on the coffee table next to an empty plate of food.

My restless heart settles a little bit. She's been looked after, and I'm thankful for that.

On the TV, a woman with blonde hair sings about a

smelly cat, and Lily and Scarlett crack up laughing. Her neck tilts back, showing off her delicate skin.

Scarlett was beautiful when she was feisty, but when she laughs, she looks like a fucking angel.

She must feel my eyes on her because she turns to the door. Her smile widens when she sees me, and knowing that she's happy to see me sends a jolt to my heart.

"Anyone give you trouble today?"

She shakes her head. "I've been fed and entertained and given hot chocolate to drink…"

"Good. Thanks, Lily, for keeping Scarlett company."

Lily rolls her eyes at me. She's the only person who can get away with that. "You make it sound like a chore, Dad."

Lily stands up and yawns and makes her excuses to leave, and a few moments later, I'm alone with Scarlett.

"How's the ankle?"

I crouch next to her, and she smells like flowers and leather—her bodywash combined with my cut—and it's a heady mix that makes my dick lengthen.

"It feels better."

It's been wrapped up in a bandage. Gina's handiwork, I'd guess.

She shuffles forward in the chair to stand up, but before she can, I scoop her into my arms.

"I can walk, you know," she says indignantly.

But she snuggles into my chest and doesn't put up a fight as I carry her back to our room. I don't live at the club-house, but this room's mine whenever I need it.

Lily must have lent Scarlett some clothes because she's in a different t-shirt under my cut and she smells fresh, like she had a shower.

"They've been looking after you all right?"

"For a prisoner, yeah. Gina's a sweetheart, and Lily's a lot of fun."

My brow furrows at the reminder that Scarlett is here against her will. But the way she's clinging onto my neck gives me hope that she wants to be here.

We reach the room, and I set her down on the end of the bed. Lily's left out an oversized t-shirt for her to wear to bed and I hand it to her.

"You can change in the bathroom. I won't look."

There's a flicker of disappointment in her eyes. But even though I'm aching to claim Scarlett, I won't do that until I know she wants me the way I want her: forever.

When she comes out of the bathroom, the over-sized shirt is clinging to her breasts and rides halfway up her thighs.

Blood thunders in my veins as my eyes rove over her body and come to rest on her lips. She's biting her lower lip, creating teeth marks on the delicate skin. I turn away before I do something that turns me into the brute she fears.

"You take the bed, honey." My voice is gravelly as I saunter over to the armchair.

"Where will you sleep?" She sticks her lip out like a petulant child, making my cock jump in my pants.

"I'll sleep right here." I tap a hand on the back of the armchair. It's too low and my back will ache in the morning, but I don't tell Scarlett that. "Where I can watch over you."

She fiddles with the bottom of her t-shirt. "You can sleep in the bed with me if you want."

Fuck. A growl escapes my lips and my cock pushes

against my zipper. She's the picture of innocence, and I want to destroy her.

"I don't think that's a good idea, honey."

"Why not?" She takes a step closer until she's standing before me, her chin jutting out defiantly and the fire returning to her eyes.

I capture her chin in my hand, and my thumb runs over her smooth skin.

"Because if I get into that bed with you, I won't be able to control myself."

Her breathing becomes heavy and her nipples harden, pressing against the thin cotton of her t-shirt.

"Maybe that's what I want."

Her words come out breathy and send a jolt through my body. She's offering herself to me. It would be the ultimate revenge to take the innocence of my rival's daughter.

But I won't use Scarlett like that, no matter how much I want to.

When I take her, it'll be after I've taken my revenge, and knowing that she wants to be here. But with what I have planned for her father, she won't want anything to do with me.

Her hand reaches for me tentatively until she strokes the hardness pressed against my jeans.

"Scarlett..." I groan a warning, but her hand's sliding up and down my bulge and I've never wanted a release so badly.

"Are you a virgin?"

Her hand stops, and a pink tinge colors her cheeks. "Yes." She looks down as if she's embarrassed.

Fuck, I thought so. It makes me want her more, and it

also makes it more impossible to take her now. But that doesn't mean I can't give her some release.

Without warning, I engulf her in my arms and lift her off the floor. She squeaks in surprise as I carry her to the bed.

"I'm not going to take your virginity yet." I lay her down on the bed, and her hair fans out on the pillow.

"But I am going to taste that sweet pussy."

She gasps as my hand slides up her thighs. She's woken the beast inside me, and I won't stop until I have her clit dancing on my tongue.

My mouth crashes into hers, and it's not gentle this time. It's needy and hungry, my tongue pushing into her, claiming her mouth as my fingers slide between her slick folds.

She gasps and wiggles underneath me. I pull back, my hand freezing in her panties.

"Don't stop," she moans.

"You sure you want this?" I duck my head so I'm looking her in the eye. "You stop anytime you want, okay? I'm not a brute, Scarlett. You control this."

She nods, and that's all I need to keep going.

"Take that off." She obeys, pulling the t-shirt over her head, revealing perky breasts and hard nipples.

I palm her tits, my mouth sucking in a nipple and my stubble grazing her skin. She moans and writhes under me, and I almost shoot my load in my pants. I'm the luckiest motherfucker in the whole damn world to have this woman wriggling under me.

My mouth travels south until I wrap my lips around her most sensitive nub. Her hips arch and she bucks under me, and while she does, I drive a finger home. She comes hard and fast, her hands tangling in my hair. She's gasping for breath, but I'm not done yet.

My tongue flicks her bud until she's writhing again, calling out my name as she comes again and again.

Somewhere between the second and sixth orgasm I pull my aching dick out of my pants and fist myself, getting off on the taste of her.

I've lost count of how many times Scarlett comes, but I can't hold back any longer. The next time her pussy convulses around my finger, I let myself go, pulling my dick out to squirt hot cum over her thighs and trembling pussy. My seed gushes out in thick ropes, coating her pink folds and marking her as mine.

I may not have claimed Scarlett yet, but I've marked her as mine. Mine, mine, mine. For now, and forever.

We fall exhausted onto the bed, and she's so tired that she falls asleep easily in my arms.

I kiss her hair and breathe in her sweet scent. But sleep eludes me. My thoughts have gone to her father, what I have to do tomorrow, and how much Scarlett will hate me afterwards.

8
SCARLETT

I wake from the best sleep I've had in as long as I can remember. Bruno's arm is draped over me, and I love the casualness of it, how we fit together even when we're sleeping.

Bruno stirs and pulls me closer to him. Something digs into my back, and I gasp when I realize it's his hard dick. Memories of last night flood my brain, his wicked tongue and the way I rode it shamelessly.

Heat flushes my neck, and I don't know if I'm embarrassed that I let myself go or frustrated because I want to do it again.

"Morning, beautiful."

Bruno brushes his stubbly chin against my neck, causing a flicker of desire to uncoil in my belly. I could get used to this, to waking up in Bruno's arms and being called beautiful and living here amongst people who are supposed to be my enemies but look after me better than my own club does.

"Did you sleep well?"

Bruno snakes his hand up my stomach and cups my breast in his palm. My nipples scrape against his fingers, and I arch my back into him, hoping he'll succumb to his need and take me.

There's a knock at the door, and Bruno's hand pauses on my breast.

"What is it?" he snaps.

"It's time, Pres," comes a muffled voice from the other side of the door.

Bruno checks his watch. "Shit. I overslept."

He plants a kiss on my shoulder and slides out of bed. "That's what you do to me, sweetheart. You make me lose track of time."

My heart flutters. Do I really have this effect on this big, powerful man? I push back on my elbows and the blanket slides off my shoulder, tickling my nipples as it slips down to pool around my waist. Bruno makes a strangled sound, and I push my tits forward, loving the hungry way he's looking at me. Is it wrong that I want him to devour me?

In one stride, Bruno's kneeling by the bed with my nipple in his mouth. I let out a squeal of surprise, then giggle in embarrassment that whoever's behind the door will have heard me.

"I'll be there in ten minutes," Bruno calls out before turning his attention back to my nipples.

"You'll be the death of me, sweetheart."

He burrows under the blanket, and I lie back as his tongue gets to work, my mind going blank as pleasure overwhelms me.

I don't even last ten minutes. It's less than a minute

before I'm gripping his hair and calling out his name, not caring who hears us anymore.

Bruno fists his cock, and this time, I wiggle down the bed and take him in my mouth before he can come.

I love his wide-eyed look of surprise and the moment he gives into pleasure and lets me take him in my mouth.

I don't know what I'm doing, but instinct kicks in as I suck and lick. Then he's coming, hot liquid burning my throat. I swallow him down as he groans my name.

He tilts my head up, and I let him slide out of my mouth.

"Was that okay?"

"Oh, honey…"

There's another knock on the door, and I guess our ten minutes are up.

"I'm coming," Bruno growls.

He straightens up and pulls his pants on.

I don't show him my disappointment. I know how clubs work. When there's a job to do, you got to do it, especially as the president. People are relying on Bruno.

He dresses quickly, and I prop myself up in bed to watch. Bruno might be twice my age, but his body is lean and muscular, patterned with scars and tattoos—artwork that I'm aching to explore.

By the time he's dressed, the relaxed look he woke up with is gone, replaced by a grim expression. His eyes are hard, his mouth a thin line.

A bolt of fear pierces my heart as suspicion sears through me.

"Where are you going?"

Bruno finishes doing up his belt buckle and doesn't answer.

"You're going to see my father, aren't you?"

The way his eyes dart to the door confirms my suspicion.

"Bruno?" I swing my feet out of bed, only slightly wincing at my sore ankle. I pull my t-shirt over my head and reach Bruno before he gets to the door.

"You're not going to hurt him, are you?"

Bruno drags in a deep breath. "Your father is responsible for putting me inside. He ratted me out to the cops."

I recoil at his words. It's the worst thing you can do in our world, speaking to the cops. Even ratting on an enemy breaks the strict moral code.

"Dad would never rat."

Bruno puts his hands on my shoulders. "My intel inside all pointed to your father. I'm sorry."

My stomach clenches, and fear for my father fills my heart. I know what happens to rats.

"But it couldn't have been him. He's not a bad man."

I don't like the way Bruno's looking at me. He's cold and distant, like I don't know him, like we didn't share last night together.

"Please…" I hate begging, but the thought of my father hurting makes my heart ache. He may not have protected me like he should have, but he's the only family I've got.

"Please don't hurt him."

Bruno's eyes flicker, and I think maybe, just maybe, I'm getting through to him.

"At least talk to him first, hear his side. I'm sure it couldn't have been him.

Bruno stares at me and I can't read his expression. He drops my arms and runs a hand through my hair.

There's a knock at the door, this time more urgent. "Pres…"

Bruno pulls the door open. "Change of plan. Organize a meeting with Manny."

Relief floods me as Bruno cups my chin. "For the last three years, all I've thought about is revenge. But one night with you, Scarlett, and my heart's gone soft."

He kisses me hard and disappears out the door.

I only hope like hell that I'm right about my dad.

9

BRUNO

My body's taut with tension as I turn my bike onto the dirt road that leads to the meeting place. The reassuring thunder of my men behind me does nothing to ease the conflict that's going through my mind.

For three years, all I've thought about is revenge. Now Scarlett's pleading look makes me question my motives. What will I gain if I take Manny out? I'll lose the woman I love, and for what?

Manny's already here, pacing the dirt track in front of where his men's bikes are lined up under the trees.

"Where is she?" Manny snarls as soon as I'm off my bike.

"She's safe. I wouldn't hurt a woman."

"Show me." He advances toward me, his face pinched. And if it wasn't for Scarlett, I'd pummel his face into oblivion.

"It's thanks to her that we're having this chat, so I'd calm down if I were you." I keep my voice level, exuding a calmness I don't feel.

"If you've laid a hand on her..."

Manny's eyes are wild, and it suddenly dawns on me. He's here for her. Only her. He's a worried father terrified for his little girl. He doesn't know about my revenge. And that gives me pause.

"What happened, Manny? Three years ago. When I got picked up. What happened?"

Manny runs his hand through his greasy hair.

"I got a call while we were on the way telling me not to go."

His gaze is steady when he says it.

"Sounds convenient."

"You think I called the cops? You think that was me?"

His eyes widen, and his shock seems genuine. "Is that what this is all about? You think I put you inside?"

He sounds incredulous, and a kernel of doubt unfurls in my stomach.

"You really think I'd do that? After everything we've been through?"

My thoughts go to the history of Manny and the Chaos Riders. We used to work together, until they got greedy and expanded into our territory. Since then, it's been competitive but never bloody, and we've never been anything more than rivals competing for the same cut of the pie.

"I swear, man. I'd never go to the cops."

He spits on the ground, showing his distaste for the corrupt officers we have around here.

"I got intel when I was inside."

His eyes narrow. "Who from? Who's trying to set me up?"

It's a good question. Who would benefit from a war between the Crows and the Riders? I got my intel from a brother I thought I could trust, but a year ago, he cut out to ride with the Reapers. They're another club up the coast and big in the drug trade, which we try to keep out of the Sunset Coast. If the Crows and the Riders weaken, it'd be easy for the Reapers to come into our territory.

I keep my thoughts to myself for now. I'll need to confirm my suspicions before any retaliation.

Manny shifts impatiently.

"I didn't go to the cops. You can believe me or not. Hell, kill me if you want to, but don't harm my little girl."

He's worried about Scarlett, which raises him in my estimation. Maybe I've had it wrong all these years.

I signal to Lyle, and he pulls open the back of the van. Scarlett blinks in the light before stepping out of the van. Her ankle makes her wobble, and she grabs the side of the van for support.

I go over and clasp her arm, and she hobbles over to her father.

He embraces her in a warm hug, and she leans into him. It's clear the affection they share for each other.

"Are you hurt? Did they hurt you, baby?"

He grips her shoulders, and his eyes flash the same danger I've seen in hers. I know he'll kill me in an instant if I've hurt his little girl. But Scarlett shakes her head.

"I twisted my ankle, but that's all. They've looked after me."

She's still wearing my cut, and I come up behind her and slide it off her shoulders. Scarlett turns around, shocked, giving me an incomprehensible look.

"You're free to go."

The look Scarlett gives me breaks my heart. But I have

to let her go. It has to be her choice. I don't think she under-stands that.

"But…" The question hangs on her lips. I know what she wants to ask me, but her eyes dart around at the men watching. She won't embarrass herself in front of them.

"I'm handing you back to your father."

Her eyes narrow, and her neck flushes with anger.

"I'm not a thing you can hand from one man to another."

Her feistiness makes me smile.

"That's not what I meant, sweetheart."

I take a step back but hold the cut up. "This will be yours when you want it. But I kidnapped you. I can't make you stay with me."

It pains me to say it because that's exactly what I want to do, but it has to be her choice. And I hope like hell she chooses me.

"Come on. Let's go." Manny wraps his arm around Scar-lett's shoulders and shuffles her toward his bike. Scarlett looks back over her shoulder, and I will her to run to me, to tell me she wants to be with me.

I hope she can see in my eyes how much I long for her.

"Wait, Dad." Manny pauses, and she half turns to him. "I love you, Daddy, but my place is with the Crows now. With Bruno.

My heart leaps as Manny's mouth drops open.

Scarlett hobbles toward me, and I meet her with my cut, sliding her arms into it and draping it over her shoulders, letting every man here know that she belongs to me and she's under my protection.

"What the fuck is this?" Manny's eyes flash dangerously,

and the tension in the air is thicker than when we first arrived.

"It's Scarlett's choice," I say smoothly. "As my old lady, she will have protection at my club. I don't put up with any shit toward any woman." I eye his men pointedly, and some of them look away, unable to meet my gaze.

Manny glares at his men, and I wonder how much he knows about what's been going on. He must realize she'll be safer with me and that he doesn't have a choice in the matter because he steps back.

What he does next I couldn't tell you because I have eyes only for Scarlett.

She slides onto the back of my bike and wraps her arms tight around me. Not bound this time—by choice.

"Where to, honey?"

"Oh, you know where. We have unfinished business in the bedroom."

My bike purrs to life, and I speed off, my dick already lengthening with the press of her body behind me.

I'm taking her home to claim my woman.

SCARLETT

*M*y thighs wrap around Bruno and my chest presses into his back. With the hum of the bike under my thighs, I'm already dripping with need by the time we speed past the clubhouse.

Bruno takes me out of town, and I guess we're going to his place. We cut off the highway and snake along a winding road that climbs into the cliffs. The road climbs higher and higher until we reach the crest, and Bruno pulls into a driveway with a modest house of dark wood perched on the cliff face.

He cuts the engine and I sit back, admiring the view. The whole bay is spread out before us with the vast ocean disappearing into the horizon.

"It's beautiful."

"It's your new home."

His hand clasps mine as he leads me inside. The entryway opens to a living room with floor-to-ceiling windows, and I catch my breath at the view. The ocean sparkles below us, boats like miniatures riding the sea.

Bruno stands behind me, and his hot breath skims my neck. "It's your home now, Scarlett."

My body quivers in response, and I don't know if it's from the feeling of coming home or his lips grazing my neck.

Bruno's hand slides around my middle, and he pulls me backward until I'm pressed against him, his hardness rubbing up against me.

"Everything I have, I give to you."

As he says the words, his mouth kisses my neck, and his hands work at my jeans until they fall to the floor.

He marches me forward and spreads my legs so my arms rest on the glass. All the while his hands explore me, slipping my panties off and running his fingers over my slick folds.

"You're so wet for me, honey."

Bruno grunts in satisfaction, and I push my ass back as I wiggle it against him. There's a hum of desire coming from between my legs, and I push back into him, needing to feel some friction.

Bruno meets me with his hand as he sinks to his knees behind me.

"What are you do—" My sentence finishes with a yelp as his finger slips inside me and his tongue grazes my back entrance.

It shouldn't feel this good, but I push my ass out, wanting more.

Bruno chuckles, sending warm breath to tickle every opening. "I want to see you come for me, honey."

He pushes my legs apart and licks me from entrance to entrance. My body shivers, and a whimper escapes my lips.

I look down at the people below us, the specks on the beach that could look up at any moment and see what we're up to. The thought makes it more intense, and my body flushes with desire. I want them to look. I want someone to be on their boat with binoculars watching the president of the Underground Crows eat me out.

I spread my thighs to give him maximum access and push my ass out so his tongue reaches my clit. But it's not my nub he's hungry for.

While Bruno's fingers work my needy pussy, his tongue flicks my puckered entrance, causing all sorts of sensations I never knew possible. It's so dirty that it doesn't take long for my climax to build.

"I'm gonna come," I whine, and Bruno presses harder, building an impossible pressure that explodes all over his face and fingers.

I cry out, my fists slick with sweat on the glass.

My legs are trembling as Bruno takes my hand and leads me down a corridor to the master bedroom. A four-poster bed stands in the middle of the room, and it's even plusher than the clubhouse. But I don't have time to admire the decor.

We tear at each other, ripping off our remaining clothes. Our mouths tangle in an intense kiss until we flop onto the bed, naked and panting.

My eyes widen when I see Bruno's length, thick and long with a purple vein throbbing at the base and a pearly bead of precum hanging off the tip.

My insides clench, wondering how I'm going to fit him inside of me. Bruno must read my thoughts because he takes my chin in is hand.

"Don't look so worried, honey. You were made for me."

"But I haven't done this before."

Bruno's eyes burn with lust, and his voice comes out like gravel. "You were made for me, Scarlett. You'll take all of me."

It's as much a command as a reassurance, and desire pools in my core. I love it when he's commanding, telling me what to do. Bruno kneels before me, his hand around the base of his beast. I lie back and try to relax, but a tension that wasn't there a few moments ago runs up my body.

Bruno's hand caresses my thighs. "We'll take it slow. I'll look after you."

His hands move up my body, and he shimmies up the bed until he's over me, pinning me down like that first night when I attacked him. His eyes are level with mine, and they're full of desire and something else, something deeper.

"I love you, Scarlett."

The words make my body relax and my heart soar.

"I love you too, Bruno."

He kisses me softly, tenderly as he lowers his hard body against mine. His thighs push mine apart and his length nestles between my legs. I feel it throbbing against my skin, and I wiggle under him until it's pulsing against my pussy lips.

We move slowly. Bruno rotates his hips, causing his cock to slide against my pussy, until I'm so swollen with need that I take his cock and guide it into place.

He pushes at my entrance, and this time, I'm ready. I open for him, and he thrusts inside, plunging into me.

There's a searing pain and I buck away, but Bruno grabs my hips and welds himself to me.

"Stay with me, honey. The pain will pass. Keep your eyes on me."

My eyes are scrunched up, and I ease them open. Bruno's staring at me, love shining out through his very soul.

"I had darkness in my heart until I found you, Scarlett. I came looking for revenge, but I found love instead."

As he says the words, he rocks slowly, and the pain subsides. Now I feel full, fuller than I ever have—full of the man I love.

My legs wrap around his waist, and I cry out as he goes even deeper. Bruno rocks slowly until my body fully relaxes and the first fingers of pleasure unfurl in my loins.

Our bodies move together, and my breasts press against his chest, slick with our combined sweat. And this is love. This is togetherness, and I know in this moment that I'll always be loved and protected.

"Bruno!" I cry as my climax peaks. He pumps hard and explodes with me.

My vision blurs and I see stars, clinging to him as our bodies rock together.

"I love you," he repeats and repeats until the words are emblazoned on my heart.

Afterwards, he pulls me close, and we lie together, our bodies fitting perfectly. I fall asleep knowing I'm safe and protected and, above all, loved.

EPILOGUE

BRUNO

Three years later…

The sounds of a baby giggling pull me out of a deep sleep. My eyes flutter open, and the first thing I see is my wife. She's nestled in the feeding chair, rocking slowly with her nursing top hanging open on one side. Her hair falls over her shoulder, and our daughter Ana pulls at it with tubby fingers.

Scarlett smiles down at Ana. With the morning sun on her face, she looks like an angel sent down from Heaven. I utter up a silent prayer of gratitude to whoever's listening because I'm the luckiest motherfucker in the whole damn world.

Scarlett must feel my eyes on her because she looks up, her smile turning to a frown when she sees that I'm awake.

"Sorry, I tried not to wake you."

"Don't be sorry, honey."

I pull myself out of bed as Scarlett pulls down the other side of her top. Her breasts are swollen with milk, and my dick twitches at the sight. Scarlett doesn't miss the movement. It's pretty hard to when I sleep naked. Her eyebrows raise, and she gives me a warning look.

"These aren't for you right now."

Ana suckles on her breast, and Scarlett leans her head back on the back of the chair. There are dark circles under her eyes, but she wears a contended smile. Motherhood suits her, and as soon as she's ready, I'll plant another baby in her belly.

"You coming to lunch today?"

Scarlett and Ana always go visit her father on Sundays. Sometimes I go with them when there's no club business. It started as an awkward meal with Manny and I eyeing each other over the table, but over the last three years, we've both mellowed. The arrival of Ana has helped. I've seen a soft side to the old bastard now that he's a grandpa.

It's made our business dealings a lot smoother. The clubs work together to everyone's benefit. Marrying Scarlett was the best thing I ever did in more ways than one. I married the woman I love, and it brokered a peace with the Chaos Riders, like a royal fucking alliance.

I kiss Scarlett on the head on my way past her to the shower.

My dick's sticking straight out, but I don't push her. She's an exhausted mother, and I can be patient if I need to be.

I start the shower and step under the hot water, letting it wash away the night's sleep. A few minutes later, the door to the ensuite opens. Scarlett's naked, her body as curvy and soft as ever, made softer by motherhood.

"Ana's gone down for a nap…"

She steps slowly into the shower, trailing her finger through the condensation on the glass. My dick perks up knowing the sweet treat that's coming my way.

We don't get as many moments alone since the baby came along, but that means we treasure the ones we do get that much more.

I've got a few moments alone with my wife, and I don't intend to waste them.

WHAT TO READ NEXT

THE BIKER'S CURVY VALENTINE

She wandered in off the street and straight into my heart...

I found her wandering the highway on Valentine's Day, barefoot with torn clothes. She doesn't remember who she is, where she came from, or who gave her the bruises on her body.

I call her Valentine because that's the day she wandered into my life—the day my life changed forever.

Valentine doesn't remember her past, but that doesn't mean she doesn't have one. And when it comes for her, I'll do whatever it takes to protect my Valentine.

The Biker's Curvy Valentine is an age-gap, amnesia, instalove romance featuring an OTT obsessed ex-military hero and the curvy woman he'll do anything to protect.

Keep reading for an exclusive excerpt or go to:
mybook.to/UCBikersCurvyValentine

THE BIKER'S CURVY VALENTINE

CHAPTER ONE

Lyle

Salt air stings my lips, and the wind whips against my cheeks as I speed away from the clubhouse. Gina's decorating for the Valentine's party, and it's the last place I want to be right now.

It seems everyone's finding love apart from me, and I don't need a shitty holiday to remind me of my single status. It's been me and my bike for forty-two years. If I haven't found a woman by now, I doubt I ever will.

As the lines of the highway blur beneath me, my mind clears. It's just me and the road. Just the way I like it.

I lock into a cruising speed, taking it easy and enjoying the scenery, the ocean on one side and orange cliffs on the other. A pickup toots as it passes me, and I give them a friendly wave. When I'm riding wearing my cut, people are either extra friendly on the roads or extra assholey. Today I'm getting all tooting horns and smiles.

I come 'round a bend in the road, and there's a long

straight stretch in front of me. Up ahead there's a dark smudge moving along the side of the road, and as I get closer, I make out that it's a person.

Some crazy fucker is walking up the highway. There's no hard shoulder and definitely no footpath. Some fucking idiot is taking their life into their hands.

As I get closer, I see that it's a woman. Her black clothes are dusty and she's barefoot. Something don't look right.

I pull over into the narrow sideling in front of her and cut the engine.

"Hey, you okay?"

She doesn't look up as I slide off the bike and start toward her.

The woman's concentrating on her feet, and as I get closer, I see her toes are bloody and covered in dirt.

"Holy shit."

She's wearing black leggings and an oversized shirt, both dusty from the road. Her dark hair hangs limp and tangled, her fringe plastered to her forehead in the heat.

"You okay, sweetheart?"

I stand right in front of the woman, and she stops moving, her eyes taking in my boots and slowly traveling up my body until her gaze lands on my face.

I feel a jolt in my bones as her gaze finds mine. She's beautiful, this lost woman. Bloody and dirty with the face of an angel. Her eyes are deep blue like the ocean, and her thick eyebrows are knit together as she regards me. The dirt of the road is smudged on her cheeks, and there's cracked blood on her temple.

"Did someone hurt you?"

A tremor of rage shakes my body at the thought of

someone laying a finger on this woman. I don't know her, but I feel a surge of protectiveness toward her.

She stares at me, her eyes running over my face in deep concentration.

"Do I know you?" Her voice is croaky, and she coughs after speaking as if the dust has gone right down her throat.

"No, sweetheart. I'd remember you if we'd met before."

Her face scrunches up in frustration, and she turns to stare out at the ocean. I don't understand the emotions running through her, but I do understand one thing: she needs my help.

"What's your name, honey?"

She swallows hard but doesn't answer.

"Where are you headed?" I try again.

But the woman remains looking out at the sea. It's a steep cliff here, and the waves crash relentlessly below us. Her look turns wistful, and for an awful moment, I think she's going to jump.

I grab her arm, making sure she doesn't, and she flinches. Her head ducks and her other arm comes up protectively to cover her head.

The action makes my heart break and my blood boil.

"Did someone hurt you?"

I crouch down so I'm lower than her eye level, less threatening. I know how intimidating I can look with my cut on and my tattoos.

"I'm not going to hurt you, sweetheart. But I'd like to help you if you'll let me."

She drops her arms but keeps looking at her feet.

"My name's Lyle. I'm ex-military," I tell her because that usually softens people's opinions about me. "I'd like to take you somewhere safe where we can get you some food and water and someone can take a look at that cut on your head."

She doesn't say anything, so I push on. I don't want to take her anywhere against her will, but it's clear this woman needs help.

"What's your name, honey?"

She mumbles something that I don't quite catch. I lean forward, and I'm so close her hair tickles my neck. She smells of the road and, underneath that, a sweet scent that's all her. I bet that even if she washed a hundred times, she'd still smell like it.

"I didn't get that. What's your name?"

She tips her head up, and suddenly we're looking into each other's eyes, so close I could kiss her dust covered lips.

"I don't know."

Her voice comes out as a gravelly whisper, and there's a flash of terror and confusion in her face. I'm wondering what the fuck is going on here.

"You don't know your name?"

She shakes her head, her brows sliding together as she looks at her feet. "I don't remember."

She turns her pleading eyes toward me. She's scared and she's vulnerable. I'm fucking angry that no one else has stopped to help her. By the looks of her feet, she's been walking all fucking day, maybe longer. But I'm also relived that I was the one to find her.

"Okay, sweetheart. I'm going to take you to the club-house and get you some help. Is that okay with you?"

She nods slightly and looks relieved, which makes my

chest swell with a protectiveness that I've never felt before. This woman needs my help. She needs my protection.

"You ever been on a bike before?"

She glances behind me to my Harley pulled up on the side of the road. The look of concentration returns to her face, and after a few moments, she shakes her head.

"I don't know."

This woman doesn't know who she is or where she's going. She doesn't even know her own name.

I should take her to the hospital. I should take her to the police. But as she slides onto the back of my bike and her little hands wrap around my waist, she leans her head on my back and gives a little sigh of relief. I know there's no way I'm taking her anywhere but to my clubhouse. Whoever she is, wherever she came from, she's mine now.

Available from Amazon or visit:
mybook.to/UCBikersCurvyValentine

GET YOUR FREE BOOK

Sign up to the Sadie King mailing list for a FREE book! You'll be the first to hear about exclusive offers, bonus content and all the news from Sadie King.

I see her on stage, and I know she'll be mine...

The Biker's Private Dancer is an age gap, MC-lite short and steamy instalove romance featuring an OTT possessive biker and a curvy girl with a secret.

The Biker's Private Dancer is a bonus book in the Underground Crows MC series available exclusively to Sadie King email subscribers.

To claim your free copy visit:
www.authorsadieking.com/free

BOOKS BY SADIE KING

Sunset Coast

Underground Crows MC

Sunset Security

Men of the Sea

The Thief's Lover

The Henchman's Obsession

The Hitman's Redemption

Wild Heart Mountain

Mountain Heroes

Military Heroes

Wild Riders MC

Maple Springs

Men of Maple Mountain

All the Single Dads

Candy's Café

Small Town Sisters

Kings County

Kings of Fire

King's Cops

For a full list of titles check out the Sadie King website

www.authorsadieking.com

ABOUT THE AUTHOR

Sadie King is a USA Today Best Selling Author of short instalove romance.

She lives in New Zealand with her ex-military husband and raucous young son.

When she's not writing she loves catching waves with her son, running along the beach, and good wine, preferably drunk with a book in hand.

Keep in touch when you sign up for her newsletter. You'll even snag yourself a free short romance!

www.authorsadieking.com/free

Printed in Great Britain
by Amazon

47630898R00047